The Red Donut Adventure

by Charlotte Hutchins

Illustrations by Mike Motz

Inspired by my husband, Bapa Bear, who is
the best grandpa ever to our grandchildren,
and the one who has always believed in me.

Dedicated to all my children and their spouses
who give me such joy, and to my grandchildren now
and in the future who allow me to enjoy the sweetness
of childhood again and again through their wholehearted
enthusiasm and spontaneous imagination.

To my good girlfriends who have been there to
cheer me on to turn my dream into reality.

For all the families everywhere who are sheltering in
place while taking care of their little ones to keep them safe
and unafraid during the COVID-19 pandemic of 2020.

Many thanks to Mike Motz for his remarkable illustrations.

With Love, Marme Bear

"Bored, bored, bored!" says Hugh Bear.

"Yeah, me too," agrees his older brother, Henry Bear.

"What can we do when there is nothing to do?"
Mae Bear asks as their baby brother, Graham Bear,
dozes in his swing, cozy and snug.

Mae Bear, who loves drawing, painting, dancing, singing, soccer, and softball, wants to do something different today. Yet she doesn't know what she wants to do.

Henry Bear loves taking part in tee-ball, being a superhero, going on safaris, playing with Legos, and following his big sister, Mae Bear, everywhere she goes. He wants to do something different too.

Hugh Bear loves to talk and asks where "his people" are if they are not home. He likes to play with toy cars and trucks in the dirt, jump on the trampoline, shoot hoops with Daddy Bear, and roast marshmallows over the fire pit with his family. Once again, it is snowing outside, and Hugh Bear can't do the things he likes to do most. He wants to do something different, but what?

Graham Bear, too little to be bored as a small cub,
sleeps and eats, sleeps and eats, sleeps and eats.

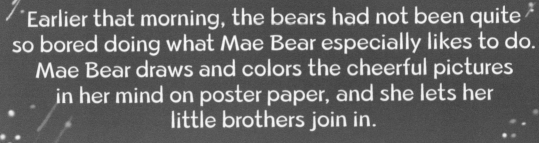

Earlier that morning, the bears had not been quite so bored doing what Mae Bear especially likes to do. Mae Bear draws and colors the cheerful pictures in her mind on poster paper, and she lets her little brothers join in.

Henry Bear, happy to be included, does not mind when Mae Bear reaches for the same crayon that he does as long as he has another one.

Hugh Bear is content creating his very own picture
with as many crayons as he can put into his little paws.
He doesn't care whether the other two have a
tug-of-war over the same crayon once in a while.

As soon as the three bears tape their pretty pictures of sun and water to the wall, they wish they were at the beach. They are bored, bored, bored.

The long wintry days are too cold, too wet, and too windy
to play outdoors in the slushy snow, so they are stuck,
stuck, stuck inside with nothing to do.

Suddenly, Mae Bear is struck with an idea: she imagines sailing away to a faraway island! Could they? Would they? How are they going to get there, and how long will it take to go and come back?

Of course, the bears do not have money for plane tickets. Mae Bear remembers dreamily that their good friend, Sam Bear, sails around the world on an inflatable ring that looks like a red donut. What if they can too?

Out in the cold garage, they look and look and look. Henry Bear finds the red donut that looks like Sam's high up on a hook. With the words please and thank you on each of their lips, Mae Bear, Henry Bear, and Hugh Bear cheer as Mommy Bear reaches over her head and grabs the large, inflated donut for them.

The three bears dash into the house to put on their floaties. They pack their towels, paddles, pails, and shovels. They grab some tiny fish crackers for snacks and water to drink. They even remember sunscreen while Mommy Bear puts Graham Bear down for a nap in his crib.

Mommy Bear finds them the big blue blanket.
The big blue blanket covers the carpet and
the red donut sits on top. Mae Bear,
Henry Bear, and Hugh Bear give
Mommy Bear a hug and kiss goodbye.

The bears scramble onto the red donut to find
a faraway island in the sun with their belongings in tow,
hands waving goodbye, eyes looking ahead, paddles
pressing forward, and wind pushing at their backs.

They sail away all alone on the deep, blue sea
as the calm and gentle waves carry them along.

The bears eat a few fish crackers,
giggle out loud, sing songs, splash,
soak up the sun, and giggle some more.

They make up a song as they sail:

We all live on a red donut, a red donut, a red donut;
We all live on a red donut sailing on the open sea!

The bears watch playful dolphins jump
out of the water and clap when the dolphins
do it over and over again.

At last, a sweeping wave rolls and tosses the red donut, revealing to the bears the fantasy they have been dreaming of all day. A waterfall flows into a blue-green lagoon near an island with a white sandy beach that stretches for miles. Shimmering mermaids lazily swim as the sun plays peekaboo through the branches of the palm trees. They paddle to shore, excited to play in the sand and the water.

Mae Bear, Henry Bear, and Hugh Bear create small sandcastles. Mae Bear makes an angel in the warm sand which she decides is much more fun than in the cold snow.

Henry Bear makes a sand shark and puts his superhero cape on the shark. Hugh Bear asks his sister and brother for help to dig a big hole deep enough for him to get in. They do, and he does.

No longer bored, Mae Bear, Henry Bear, and Hugh Bear run and play, sing and dance, giggle and laugh.

They make friends with
Mr. and Mrs. Crab,
who are not crabby at all.

The three bears feed the seagulls the rest of their fish crackers, and closely watch an unhurried sea turtle crawl into the shallow water and swim away.

They decide to swim to the waterfall to play
with the dazzling mermaids. Henry Bear
and Hugh Bear wear their floaties to be safe.

The sun makes the three bears sleepy as they stretch out on their bright beach towels to dry. They know it is nearly time to go home.

The bears are sad to leave this beautiful place and their kind, new friends. Still they know they must not be gone too long because Graham Bear will wake up and miss them.

The bears gather all of their belongings and hop onto the red donut. Together, they paddle smoothly with the ocean current and return in time for Mommy Bear to call them to lunch.

Graham Bear wakes up from his long nap to eat and eat and eat as he sits in his highchair, not knowing his sister and brothers have just come back from a great adventure.

During lunch, Mommy Bear asks Mae Bear, Henry Bear, and Hugh Bear if they like sailing on their red donut in the blue sea, and they all happily say, "Yes, yes, yes."

The three bears invite Mommy Bear and Graham Bear to come along next time. "We would love to join in the fun, but we will need another donut," Mommy Bear says. Mae Bear shouts with delight that she would like a pink one with sprinkles on top!

Questions to Ponder:

Where have you pretended to go on your adventurous days when it is rainy or snowy outside and you cannot go out to play?

Who will join you on your adventure?

What will you bring with you?

Where do you imagine Mae Bear, Henry Bear, Hugh Bear, and Graham Bear will go on their next adventure?

What do many bears actually do in the winter?

Many of the Pre-K through Third Grade Dolch Sight Words are in this book.
How many can you find as you read?

- **Pre-Kindergarten Dolch Sight Words** (40 words) a, and, away, big, blue, can, come, down, find, for, funny, go, help, here, I, in, is, it, jump, little, look, make, me, my, not, one, play, red, run, said, see, the, three, to, two, up, we, where, yellow, you

- **Kindergarten Dolch Sight Words** (52 words) all, am, are, at, ate, be, black, brown, but, came, did, do, eat, four, get, good, have, he, into, like, must, new, no, now, on, our, out, please, pretty, ran, ride, saw, say, she, so, soon, that, there, they, this, too, under, want, was, well, went, what, white, who, will, with, yes

- **First Grade Dolch Sight Words** (41 words) after, again, an, any, as, ask, by, could, every, fly, from, give, going, had, has, her, him, his, how, just, know, let, live, may, of, old, once, open, over, put, round, some, stop, take, thank, them, then, think, walk, were, when

- **Second Grade Dolch Sight Words** (46 words) always, around, because, been, before, best, both, buy, call, cold, does, don't, fast, first, five, found, gave, goes, green, its, made, many, off, or, pull, read, right, sing, sit, sleep, tell, their, these, those, upon, us, use, very, wash, which, why, wish, work, would, write, your

- **Third Grade Dolch Sight Words** (41 words) about, better, bring, carry, clean, cut, done, draw, drink, eight, fall, far, full, got, grow, hold, hot, hurt, if, keep, kind, laugh, light, long, much, myself, never, only, own, pick, seven, shall, show, six, small, start, ten, today, together, try, warmth

Meet
Charlotte Hutchins

Charlotte Hutchins understands that sometimes it can feel like forever to wait for the sun to come out from behind the clouds to see the positive outcome of patience, perseverance, and imagination. Born in Phoenix, she graduated with a Bachelor of Arts in English from Brigham Young University and earned a Master's Degree in Reading Curriculum from Cal State East Bay. She raised her five children in Northern California where she lived for 36 years. When Charlotte's children were young, she would often spread out a blue blanket on their family room floor for picnics, reading time, and movies. Her growing family now consists of twenty-one people, including nine grandchildren.

The family loves to gather at their cabin in Lake Tahoe, the beach in Hawaii, or in the pool in their backyard, listening to Charlotte's husband, Rick, sing his song "The Red Donut" and tell tales of Sam the Bear. Charlotte and Rick have recently moved to Utah to live closer to their grandchildren in hopes to resurrect the blue blanket.

Lightning Source UK Ltd.
Milton Keynes UK
UKHW051614180920
370103UK00005B/64